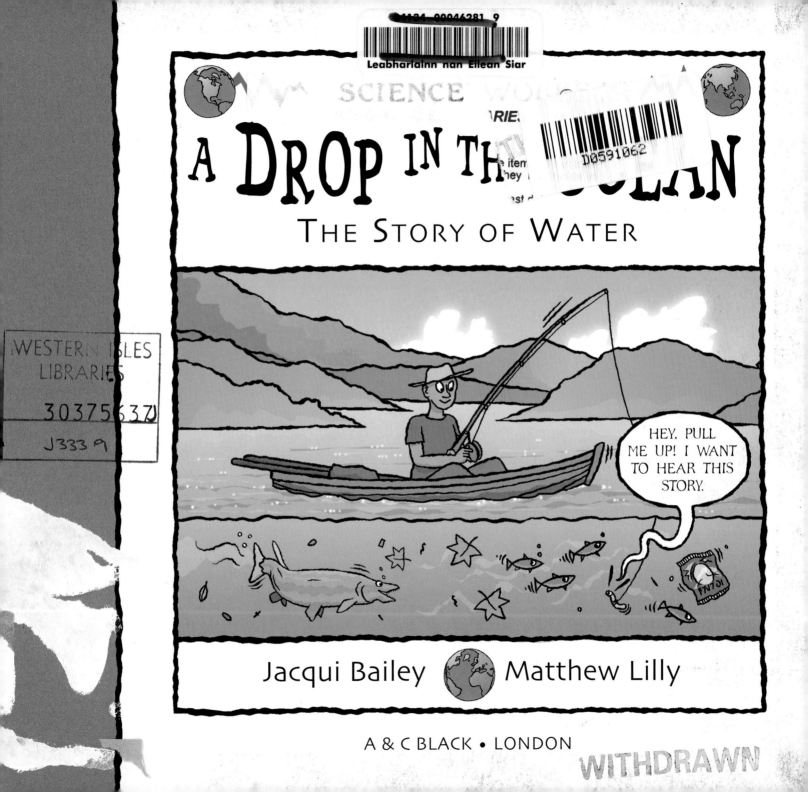

# A DROP IN THE OCEAN

## THE STORY OF WATER

Jacqui Bailey · Matthew Lilly

A & C BLACK · LONDON

Leabharlainn nan Eilean Siar

WESTERN ISLES
LIBRARIES

30375637(?)

J333 9

WITHDRAWN

Out on the great green ocean, the waves rolled and shifted and sparkled. It was a sunny day and things were hotting up.

In fact . . . the ocean's surface was so hot that tiny bits of it kept breaking away and whizzing into the air.

The water was evaporating — it was changing from a liquid into a gas, called water vapour.

ZIP!!    ZAP!    WEEEE!    ZAP!!    ZIP!!

WHAT'S GOING ON?

I DON'T KNOW, BUT I WISH I COULD DO IT.

How does that happen? Well, it's like this . . .

5

Water is a liquid and, like all liquids, it's made of billions and billions of incredibly small bits of stuff, called particles.

The particles all clump together, but each one has room to slip and slide about. This is why liquids are runny.

A water particle in liquid

WOOPS!

WEEEE!

FREE AT LAST!

A water particle in gas

But when the particles get hot they start to jiggle and jump! The hotter they get the faster they move until . . .

. . . they move so fast, they pull away from each other and float into the air. Now the particles are making a gas!

In gases, the particles try to get as far away from each other as they can. And since most particles are much too small to be seen on their own, most gases are invisible.

6

Back above the ocean, the water vapour was drifting higher and higher into the air, and spreading further and further apart.

The particles in the water vapour whizzed about — bumping and bouncing off specks of dust that also floated in the air.

7

But the higher the water vapour went, the colder the air became. The particles got cold, too, and started to cling to the specks of dust.

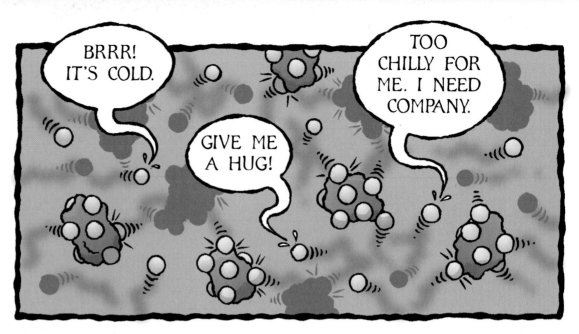

As more and more particles gathered on the dust, tiny droplets formed.

The water vapour was condensing. It was changing from a gas back into a liquid.

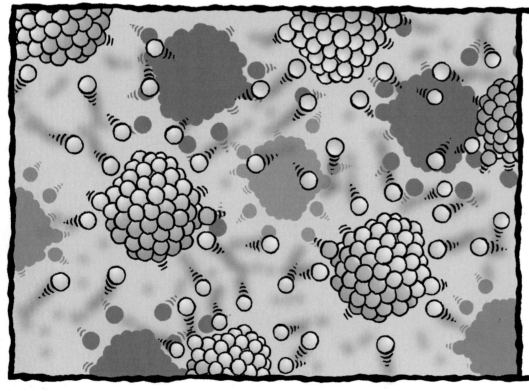

The water droplets were still very, very small, and light enough to float in the air. There were so many of them, they formed a cloud. (A cloud is just billions and billions of water droplets clumped together.)

HEY HO! HEY HO! IT'S OFF TO WORK WE GO...

A breeze came along and blew the cloud towards the shore.

As the cloud travelled, it collected more water vapour — but not from the ocean. This water vapour had evaporated from rivers, ponds, puddles and plants.

Hang on a minute — PLANTS?

Yes, that's right, plants. Plants drink loads of water. They use their roots like straws to suck up litres and litres of the stuff from the soil.

SLURP! SLURP! SLURP! SLURP! SLURP! SLURP!

WARM? I'M POSITIVELY STEAMING!

PHEW! IT'S A BIT WARM TODAY.

Then they give it back again — as water vapour oozing out through tiny holes in their leaves, especially on hot days.

By now, the cloud was stuffed full of water droplets. There were so many, they started bumping into one another.

As big droplets bashed into smaller ones, they swallowed them up.
The bigger droplets became so big . . .
and so heavy . . .
they started to fall!

The droplets had grown into raindrops.

Scientists say that a droplet becomes a raindrop when it's 0.5 mm across. That's about as big as this full stop ——→ .

Raindrops can be up to 4 mm across. That's about this big. ——→ ○
Then they usually split in two.

Some of the raindrops fell on a town. They splashed onto rooftops and roads . . .

. . . slid down pipes and gutters, and trickled into drains.

EEEEK!

SPLASH!

Inside the drains, the raindrops became a flowing rush of rainwater.

The drains carried the rainwater away from the town and emptied it into a stream.

Other raindrops made puddles and pools on the ground.

Animals came to drink from the puddles . . .

. . . and children splashed in them!

The cloud and the rain moved on. In the town, the puddles slowly disappeared. Some of the water soaked into the ground, but most of it evaporated and drifted back into the air as water vapour.

By now the cloud was floating over woodlands, fields and farmlands.

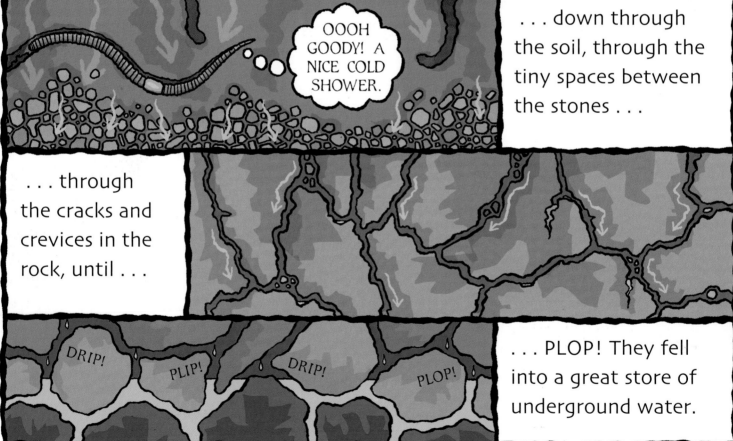

Zillions more raindrops soaked into the soil. Some were sucked up by plants, but the rest travelled on . . .

. . . down through the soil, through the tiny spaces between the stones . . .

. . . through the cracks and crevices in the rock, until . . .

. . . PLOP! They fell into a great store of underground water.

There's billions and billions of litres of water hidden under the ground. This store of water is called groundwater, and it is made by rain.

Well

Lake

Groundwater

Layer of rock or clay that water can't get through

Rain soaks down into the ground until it reaches a layer of rock or clay that's so tightly packed, it can't get through. Then it starts to fill up all the gaps and spaces in the rock and soil above (just like water fills up a sponge). The groundwater stays in the ground until either it seeps out into rivers and lakes, or people use it by digging wells.

15

Meanwhile, the cloud moved on. The wind pushed it up a mountainside.

Rain poured down and trickled over rocks and stones.

The trickles became bubbling streams, and the streams joined up to make a rushing river.

YEEEE... HAAAA!

The river bounced its way over rocks and boulders . . . flung itself over the edge of a steep drop . . . and crashed back to the river bed in a waterfall.

The river became deeper and wider. Then it turned a corner and flowed into a lake.

Not just any old lake, mind you. This lake was a reservoir — it stored water for people to drink.

But the water was too dirty to be drunk straight away. It had all sorts of stuff in it — leaves and mud, chemicals (such as the fertilisers we put on soil), and rubbish that people left behind.

There were plants and fish and all sorts of small creatures in the reservoir, too, including ones we can't see, such as germs.

So first, the water had to be cleaned.

I'M NOT DIRTY, ARE YOU DIRTY?

WHO ME? NOT ME!

17

The water was pumped into a tank and mixed with a special chemical called a coagulant (*co-ag-yoo-lant*).

COAGULANT

TEE HEE, MISSED ME!

The coagulant turned into sticky blobs that sank to the bottom of the tank, taking most of the dirt with them.

HUH! I CAN GET THROUGH THIS.

Then the water was filtered.

It slowly trickled down through a layer of small stones, and a thick layer of sand, until the water was crystal clear.

CHLORINE

AARGH, NOOO! NOT THE CHLORINE TREATMENT!

Last of all, another chemical was added to it — chlorine. The chlorine killed off any germs that had managed to get through.

In many places tiny amounts of fluoride are added to the water, too. This chemical helps to strengthen your teeth.

Finally, the clean water was pumped into big underground pipes called water mains.

From the water mains, smaller pipes carried the clean water into offices, factories, schools and homes. And there it stayed, until someone . . .

. . . took a shower,

washed some clothes,

cleaned the car,

flushed a toilet, and

drank a glass of water.

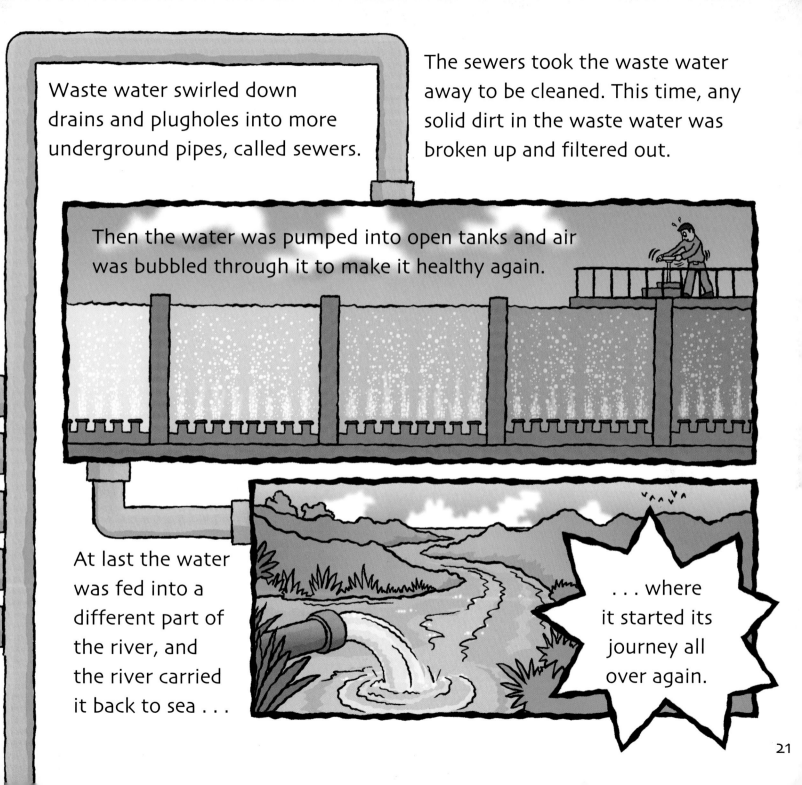

Waste water swirled down drains and plugholes into more underground pipes, called sewers.

The sewers took the waste water away to be cleaned. This time, any solid dirt in the waste water was broken up and filtered out.

Then the water was pumped into open tanks and air was bubbled through it to make it healthy again.

At last the water was fed into a different part of the river, and the river carried it back to sea . . .

. . . where it started its journey all over again.

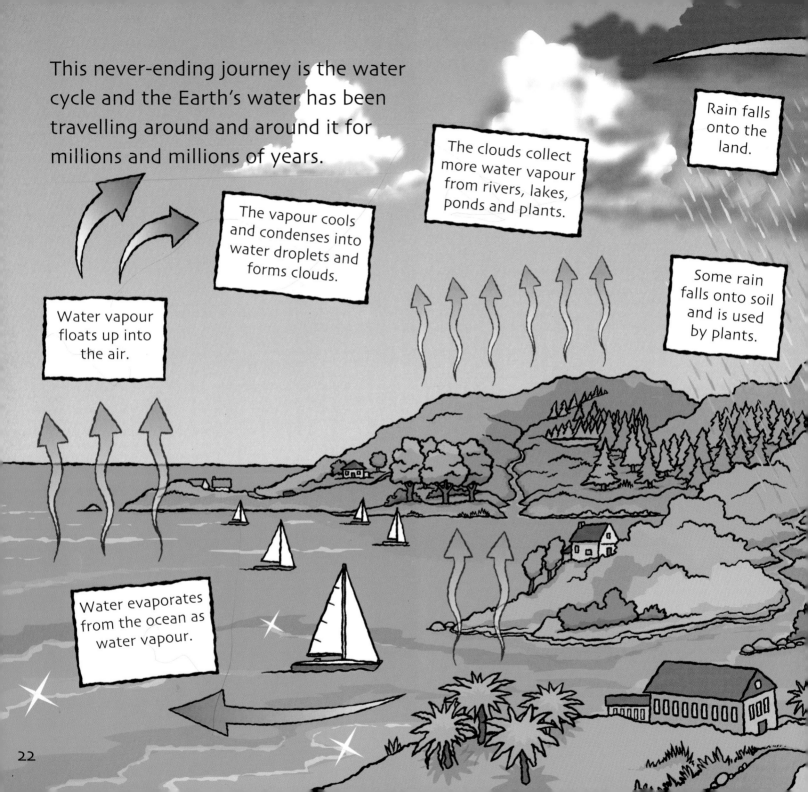

This never-ending journey is the water cycle and the Earth's water has been travelling around and around it for millions and millions of years.

The vapour cools and condenses into water droplets and forms clouds.

The clouds collect more water vapour from rivers, lakes, ponds and plants.

Rain falls onto the land.

Water vapour floats up into the air.

Some rain falls onto soil and is used by plants.

Water evaporates from the ocean as water vapour.

Some rain falls into streams and rivers.

Some rain sinks into the ground as groundwater and slowly seeps back into rivers and lakes.

People build reservoirs to collect some of the water. This water is cleaned and used by us. Afterwards, the water is cleaned again and put back into the rivers.

Streams flow into rivers and rivers flow back to the sea.

And guess what . . . the same water that was drunk by an Ancient Egyptian, or even by a dinosaur, might just have been drunk by you. Weird, but true!

# MORE GREAT STUFF TO KNOW

Without water, life on Earth couldn't exist.
But where did all the water come from in the first place?

## THE FIRST RAIN

Well, about 4 *billion* years ago the Earth was a raging hot ball of rocks, gases and not much else. One of those gases was water vapour. As the Earth slowly cooled down the water vapour condensed and it began to rain. It was the greatest rainstorm the world has ever known. When it stopped, almost three-quarters of the Earth's surface was covered with oceans — just as it is today!

## WATER, WATER, EVERYWHERE

Every living thing needs water, from a bug to a basketball player! Yet we never seem to use it up. Earth has the same amount of water now as it has always had.

But although the world has lots of water, only a tiny part of it is usable by people!

About 2 per cent of the world's water is frozen into ice (mainly at the North and South Poles).

Most of the world's water (more than 97 per cent) is in the oceans — and it's much too salty for people to drink!

Less than 1 per cent is in lakes and rivers, the soil, groundwater, and water vapour in the air. This is the only water that humans can drink.

## WHY THE SEA IS SALTY

Scientists think that once upon a time the oceans weren't salty at all. They think that most of the salt in the sea was dissolved from rocks.

Rainwater wears tiny pieces of rock away, and some of these rock pieces are salts. The rainwater carries these tiny bits of salt back to the sea. But when seawater evaporates, it leaves the salt behind.

Over billions of years, more and more salt built up in the oceans until the water became as salty as it is today.

## THE WHITE STUFF

When air is very cold, the particles in water vapour become tiny crystals of ice. When lots of crystals join together, they make a snowflake.

NICE PATTERN!

THANKS, I MADE IT MYSELF.

Snowflakes are no bigger than raindrops, but if you look at them through a magnifying glass you can see that every snowflake forms a perfect pattern, and every pattern is different.

Snowflakes melt very quickly on the ground, but on high mountaintops they can stay frozen for hundreds of years.

I'VE BEEN HERE AGES, YOU KNOW.

# TRY IT AND SEE

## THE SLUSHY STUFF

Water is magic. It can be a solid, or a liquid or a gas! It all depends on how hot or cold it gets.

Try this experiment, and make yourself a treat at the same time!

You will need:
- Small plastic yoghurt pots
- A bottle of blackcurrant or orange squash
- Lollipop sticks

**1**

Mix some squash and water together in a jug. The mixture should have about twice as much water as squash.

**2** Pour the squash into the yoghurt pots, until they are about three-quarters full. Put a stick in each pot and put the pots in a freezer. Leave them there for a few hours.

BRRR! I'M FREEZING.

What do you find when you take them out again?

The liquid has become a solid, called ice. Why? Because when water particles get very cold, they lose energy and stop moving around. Instead, they jam themselves together in a hard lump.

**3** Leave your pots out on the side and you'll soon see a difference.

WEEE! I CAN MOVE AGAIN.

The ice starts to melt back into a liquid. That's because the air in your house is warm enough to heat up the water particles (unless you live in a fridge, that is). And they're starting to slip and slide around each other again.

Let one pot melt completely. (You can eat the other ice lollies while you wait — that's the treat part!)

**4** When all the ice has melted, use a felt-tip pen to mark the level of the mixture on the lollipop stick. Now put the pot somewhere warm or sunny.

**5** Check it every now and then over the next few days. What happens to the water level? Where do you think the liquid has gone?

LOOK AT ME! I CAN FLY.

The water particles became hot and full of energy. They broke away from the rest of the liquid and floated into the air as gas.

27

# WATERY WONDERS

**1,143 cm**

The world's driest place is the Atacama Desert in Chile in South America. It has less than 1.25 cm (½ inch) of rain a year and some years it doesn't rain at all!

The Atacama does get foggy, though. And the people that live there use huge screens to condense the fog into water that they can use.

**1.25 cm**

The world's rainiest place is a mountain in Hawaii, called Mount Wai'ale'ale. On average, about 1,143 cm (450 inches) of rain falls there every year, and it rains almost every day.

Almost three-quarters of your body is made of water (about 70% of it, in fact). Even your brain is mostly made of water!

Your body loses water all the time — through sweating and going to the toilet. You need to drink at least 6 to 8 glasses of plain water (not soft drinks!) every day to replace the water you lose.

# INDEX

## SOME WATERY WEBSITES TO VISIT

www.waterinschools.com = The website belonging to Thames Water in London. Has lots of good information on water treatment and a list of great places to visit.

http://ga.water.usgs.gov/edu = The US Geological Survey's Water Science for Schools website. Contains all sorts of great info about water with lots of pics and diagrams.

www.epa.gov/safewater/kids = The US Environmental Protection Agency's website for kids. Lots of info on water treatment and conservation.

For Marie
JB

For Joanna and Raymond
ML

First published in 2003 by
A & C Black Publishers Limited
37 Soho Square, London W1D 3QZ
www.acblack.com

Created for A & C Black Publishers Limited by

two's COMPANY

Copyright © Two's Company 2003

The rights of Jacqui Bailey and Matthew Lilly
to be identified as the author and the illustrator of this
work have been asserted by them in accordance with
the Copyrights, Designs and Patents Act 1988.

A CIP record for this book is available
from the British Library. All rights reserved.
No part of this publication may be reproduced in any form
or by any means — graphic, electronic or mechanical,
including photocopying, recording, taping or information
storage and retrieval systems — without the prior
permission in writing of the publishers.

ISBN 0 7136 6255 7 (hbk)
ISBN 0 7136 6256 5 (pbk)

Printed in Hong Kong by Wing King Tong

A & C Black uses paper produced with elemental chlorine-free
pulp, harvested from managed sustainable forests.